Saviour Boy

S.L. STERLING

Untitled

Saviour Boy

The Forever Boys Series

S.L. Sterling

Saviour Boy

Copyright © 2020 by S.L. Sterling

ISBN: 978-1-989566-16-9

Paperback ISBN: 978-1-989566-17-6

Editor: Brandi Aquino, Editing Done Write

Cover Design: Thunderstruck Cover Design

Grant

I had just sat down when Gale rounded the corner, holding what appeared to be a service order.

"Grant, I'm sorry. I missed this one. It was on my desk under the orders from yesterday."

I glanced down at the work order. "Did you take this call? This order is over at a storage facility outside of town. I recognize the address. I stored my belongings there when I went overseas."

"I did. It's not the business owner either. It's for one rental locker," she said, coming around my desk. "Yes, right here. Storage locker number sixty-four," she said, pointing to where she had marked it.

"Gale, I don't think they even allow this."

"No, not normally, but the guy said he had written

permission from the business owner. He agreed to provide it to us when we were there."

"Alright, I guess I will have to be the one to go install the system then, since I gave the guys their assignments for the day." I grabbed my coffee and headed to the back of the building to get the equipment I would need.

I drove to the storage facility just on the outskirts of town and went directly to locker sixty-four. The door was open, the locker full of furniture along with a windowless white van. I put my truck into park and climbed out. I walked around to the back of my truck when a man emerged from the front passengers side of the van, raising his hand to me in greeting.

"Hey, are you the alarm guy?"

"Yep."

"You have what I ordered?"

"Sure do. Five of the best cameras and monitoring."

"Great."

"Honestly, I think five cameras is overkill for the hallway. You can get away with two for less than half the price."

"Oh, they aren't going outside the unit. They are for inside."

"Okay, but you know that cameras are to protect your stuff from being stolen, not to watch from inside."

"Yes, I know. I have something precious to me in here and just want to be sure it will be safe. So, I was going to have you put four cameras in here and one outside."

"No problem," I said, getting right to work.

The guy watched me like a hawk as I worked to install the cameras in the locations he had asked. As I got off the ladder, I backed up into a table covered with a sheet, almost knocking it over. He flew across the room, grabbing the table before I could, and glared at me.

"Please, touch nothing," he gritted as he carefully righted the table, standing and glaring at me.

I backed away slowly, and a few minutes later, I had connected the other two. I left him instructions on how to access his video feed, quickly taking a copy for my records in case, in the future, he forgot how to access them.

I watched as a sly smile crept onto his face as he pulled a wad of cash out of his pocket and paid me the twenty-five hundred dollars for the system I had just installed.

Becca

"Becca, are we keeping you from something important?" Mr. Dickson turned around and glared at me from over the rim of his glasses.

I could feel my face heating as my eyes met his. I suddenly felt like a child who had been caught doing something she shouldn't be. I glanced around as the entire boardroom lifted their heads from their notes they had been making and looked at me. I shook my head. "No, sir." I swallowed hard. "It won't happen again," I said, struggling to silence my phone, which was still vibrating on the boardroom.

"Then please, either answer whoever is messaging you and make them go away or shut your phone off," he said as my phone went off again, annoyance settling on his face.

I quickly shut the phone off, apologizing profusely for the interruption.

"Don't apologize to me, Becca. Apologize to all your co-workers who would like to learn about our spring promotions before the season kicks off. I'm also sure that most of them would like to get out of here on time for once on a Friday night, especially after the Christmas season we just had," he bit out, turning back to the whiteboard, continuing right where he had left off.

My co-workers turned their attention back to the whiteboard. I, however, sat there barely listening. I knew I should have excused myself to take that call. I could practically hear Jace's angry voice on the other end of the line. My stomach turned as the memory of what had happened just one short week ago ran vividly through my mind after not answering a call from him. I knew I should have called my brother right after it happened, but I didn't. Instead I figured he would go away if I ignored him long enough. Apparently, I was wrong.

Jace and I had been dating for the last six or seven months, until a week ago. Over the holiday season, I had come home late pretty much every single night, and he had joked about having to keep tabs on me whenever I didn't respond to his messages right away.

If I didn't answer my cell phone for whatever reason, he would call my office line, leaving messages. He would use my full name in a low and controlled voice on every message, sending chills through me.

His controlling behaviour had become irritating, but one week ago had been the breaking point. He had met me at my apartment after work last Friday night and immediately started questioning me.

"I don't understand what is so hard about answering my messages. I want to know where you've been. I've been messaging you all afternoon," Jace barked as he walked into the kitchen, stuck his head in the fridge, and pulled out a bottle of beer, while I finished chewing a handful of almonds I'd shoved into my mouth.

"I told you, I was in a meeting. I couldn't answer the phone. Mr. Dickson had been going over customer complaints, and many of those complaints concerned my department."

"I don't care. I'm important, and when I message you, I expect a response."

"I never said you weren't important, Jace, but this is my job. I didn't get the position I have by ignoring problems, and the problems he was bringing to my attention really needed to be addressed."

Jace ignored my answer and then leaned against the wall. "Fine, if you say so. Are we still heading to your parents' for the family barbecue next weekend?" he questioned, ripping the cap off his beer and guzzling half the bottle.

He had been after me for the last couple of months to take him to meet my family. He kept saying he was thinking I was ashamed of him. I assured him that wasn't the case at all. Honestly, I didn't know why I hadn't taken him home yet. Part of me felt that because I came from a long line of law enforcement, that Jace might not fit in. I knew very little about his past because he was so guarded, and I knew that my family were question-askers and answer-seekers.

"I don't think so. I have to work late on Friday and be back early Saturday. It's a long drive, and with Sunday being my only day off, it's going to be hard enough to get everything done around here."

I poured a glass of wine, putting the bottle back into the fridge. Before I could turn around, I was roughly grabbed, spun around, and brutally pushed up against the wall. I let out a deep inhale as my back and head hit the wall. It took only a second before my head began pounding, and I struggled to open my eyes.

"Rebecca, when are you going to understand I don't like being ignored. I also don't like being hidden." He glared into my eyes, his arm across my throat.

I was shaking so badly I couldn't say anything. He stood

there glaring into my eyes, his rough hand now wrapped around my throat.

"You've been running around for how long? An hour or two since the end of the workday? I've called you. You haven't returned my calls, so that means you've been ignoring me. Or are you out with someone else?" he gritted.

"Yes, it's been two hours, but..." I tried to form the words to explain I had been late because I needed to mail some stuff for work, but my head ached and I was seeing stars.

"No buts. Now I also find out you won't introduce me to your family yet again, as you promised. You say you're not ashamed of me, but it's seriously making me wonder. You say you don't ignore problems. This is a problem," he said smashing his fist into the wall beside my head, putting a significant dent in the drywall.

Never in my entire life had I ever felt the need to use my family to protect me, but I needed help. I mustered up every bit of courage I had left in me before I spoke. "Jace, do I need to remind you I come from a long line of law enforcement? My brother is ATF, my sister is DEA, and my father was FBI," I said with a shaky but calm voice.

Jace just glared at me, and then ever so slowly he let me go, straightening his shirt as he stepped back. As soon as his hands were off me, I did my best to step away and not freak out. "I think it's time you leave."

It surprised me he didn't put up a fight. Instead, he

nodded, hanging his head and, without argument, grabbed his jacket and walked out of the apartment. I ran and locked the door the second I heard it shut. That had been a week ago, and aside from the constant text messaging, I hadn't seen or heard from him.

I jumped as I felt someone pull on my arm, and I turned to see Jan, the valet manager, looking down at me. "Everything okay, Becca?" she asked, concern lining her face.

I glanced around, noticing that everyone had already packed up their notes, and aside from a few stragglers, the boardroom was almost empty.

"Yes," I said, scrambling to grab the mess of papers in front of me and put them in an unorganized pile. "I just remembered I have to do something before I leave." I practically ran towards my office, leaving Jan behind.

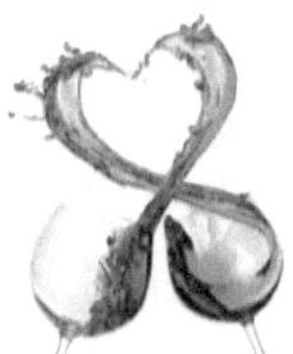

Sweat dripped from my forehead as I finished that last ten minutes of my elliptical routine. I'd needed to chase the thoughts of Jace from my memory, and the gym normally did the trick. I grabbed my towel and wiped my forehead and headed into the changing room. I quickly changed into my sweats and then headed upstairs to the wine shop to pick up my favourite bottle of Moscatto before heading home.

I now stood outside my apartment door struggling with the bottle of wine, my laptop bag, and my key. Finally, I got the key in the lock, pushed the door open, and dropped everything just inside the door. I slipped out of my sneakers and made my way into the kitchen, shoving the bottle of wine into the fridge. I grabbed a strawberry and shoved it into my mouth, then headed down the hall to the bathroom for a hot shower. Seconds later, I stood under the warm water, letting it soothe my tired, aching muscles.

When the water ran cold, I shut the taps off and reached out to grab a towel from the towel rack. Wrapping it around my body, I opened the curtain and instantly, all the tension that had left my body over the last twenty minutes was back and higher than ever as I read what was written in the condensation across the mirror. "Not Over You."

I glanced around the small bathroom, the door still closed. I felt a chill run over me. Was Jace here? How did he get into my apartment? He didn't have a key. I rushed to dry off and opened the bathroom door, poking my head out in the hallway to look around.

"Hello?" I called out. "Jace, are you here?" Silence

was all that greeted me. "This isn't funny, Jace. If you are here, say something, please."

I felt like an idiot. Of course he wasn't here. The door had been locked when I had come home, and I knew I had locked the dead bolt before I had showered. Still, another chill ran through me. I slipped across the hall into my bedroom and grabbed the phone from my nightstand. I held it in my hand for a moment, my finger tracing the number I didn't want to have to call. Yet I knew I didn't have a choice, and I dialed my brother anyway.

The phone had barely rung when his voice came across the line.

"Chris here."

"Hey, big bro. You busy?"

"Just at work. Why?"

"I need some help. Can you come over?" I knew the tremor in my voice would let him know something was wrong, and like usual, he didn't hesitate one bit.

"I'll be there in a minute."

He hadn't been kidding because within five minutes he was already banging on my door. I looked out the peephole before opening just to be sure that it was him. As soon as I saw his concerned face, I pulled the door open, and there stood my brother in all his gear.

"What's goin' on, sis? What you need my help with?" he asked, stepping into the apartment.

"Come with me," I said, pulling him in the bathroom's direction.

I pointed to the mirror as we walked into the bathroom, but the message had already disappeared as if it had never been there. "No, no, no," I cried, turning on the shower again, trying to steam up the room, but it did little good. The water was cold.

"Dammit. Why did everyone in the building have to shower now?" I mumbled.

"What is it?" he asked, frowning.

"The message. It—it's gone."

"What message? Becca, what are you talking about?" Chris looked at me with deep concern.

I blew out a breath, deciding if I should tell my brother or not. I had kept Jace a secret from my family for a reason I never knew, and I was seeing that this might have been it.

"Becca, what is it?" he asked again.

I blew out a breath and sat down on the edge of the bathtub, putting my head in my hands. "Oh, man. I started seeing this guy, Jace, six, maybe seven months ago. Things were going fine, until a week ago. He got a little violent with me in the kitchen, and I haven't heard from him since. Over the past few days, I've noticed things. He's been messaging me like crazy. I never respond, but not only that, on a number of occasions I've felt like I'm being followed. Things are being moved around my office, and today when I got out of the shower, the words _not over you_ were written on the mirror," I cried.

"Does he have a key?"

I shook my head. "No, I never gave him a key. I didn't trust him enough. Chris, what do I do?" I cried, the panic rising in me.

"Okay, well, first thing, don't panic. Did it look like anything else had been disturbed when you came home?"

I shook my head. "I don't think so. I never really paid any attention."

Chris looked around the apartment—my bedroom, the kitchen where he ran his hand over the dent in the drywall, and in closets before he took a seat on the couch. "All right, get in touch with the building's super and have the locks changed immediately, just in case he got hold of one of your keys and had a copy made."

I nodded, making a mental note to do that in the morning as my brother started checking windows and the sliding door to the balcony in both the living room and my bedroom. "You keep these doors locked all the time, right?"

"Yep, along with the one in my bedroom."

He fiddled with the little lock on the door, managing to open it while it was locked. "These locks are shit. They are really easy to open. Burglars can open most with a credit card if they do it correctly. Do you have an old broom or mop handle you can place down into the track?"

I nodded. "I will just take them off the broom and mop," I said, rushing to the utility closet and removing both and laying them in the track of the doors.

"Okay, leave it with me. I'm going to look into getting you a security system too."

I nodded as I got up and followed my brother to the door. "Thanks, Chris."

"No problem. Get some sleep," he said, kissing my forehead before he left the apartment. "If you notice anything else, just call me. After eight, I will be at home. Call the super tonight, too. These locks need to be changed tomorrow morning. If he gives you flack, I'll come do it."

"Thanks," I said, giving my brother a hug.

Grant

Johnnie's laugh was loud and clear as he finished telling us one of his usual jokes. His laugh was the last thing I remembered when the explosion sounded. We'd driven off the road and over a land mine, sending us and the MRAP flying. I braced myself, but not good enough. I felt every roll. I could hear the other guys screaming for help, and when the vehicle finally stopped rolling, that was when I felt the searing pain.

I was just about to call out when I bolted up. I glanced around the room. It took me a minute to slow my breathing and realize I was in my bed, the early-morning light of the day was just peeking through the blinds. I ran my hands over my face. I was covered in sweat and my head ached. I reached for the bottle of prescription medication, but the pain that shot down my armed stopped me. I persisted and grabbed the little bottle I had picked up from the pharmacy the day before. I quickly popped two pills and took a drink of the water that sat on my bedside table before lying back down. At first, I stared at the ceiling, and then I closed my eyes and steadied my breathing the way they had taught me to do in therapy upon realizing it had just been a bad dream.

I'd had many bad dreams over the past year. You would, too, if your MRAP hit an IED and sent you and your team flying. We lost three of our guys that day; the others had minor injuries and recovered in a field hospital. I had been airlifted to Germany where I found I had undergone surgery to fix the broken leg I had received when I had gotten pinned in the MRAP. Figuring that was the worst of my injuries, I knew I would recover, and with a little therapy, I would be back in the field, until the doctor who was caring for me came in and I tried to sit up.

· · ·

Searing pain in my neck, back, and shoulder stopped me quickly. He explained to me that there were bone and shrapnel fragments that were inoperable because of their placement. Ten very long minutes later, I'd learned that my recovery was going to be hell, but I was still ready to fight and get back to what I loved doing. Then he pulled out my x-rays and crushed all dreams I held of getting back to normal. He told me I would be discharged from the career I loved. All because of some tiny pieces of shrapnel near my spine.

At first, I'd been angry, but after nine months of intense physical and mental therapy, I was discharged from the hospital. My best friend, Chris, visited many times during my time in the hospital. When it had come time to leave, he picked me up, and together we returned to our hometown of Merlot, CA.

I struggled for a bit, trying to adjust to my new life with little to no idea of what I was going to do for work. One night, I'd been over at Chris's house when he suggested I open up a security company. At first, I thought it was a bad idea, but after a few months, I put the plan into motion and finally opened the doors. The security company idea had been one of Chris's better ideas. It had taken off, and soon I had more work than my crew could handle.

I'd just finished handing out all the work assignments for the day and gathered the remaining work orders that probably wouldn't get done until tomorrow. I had finally poured myself my first cup of coffee of the day and had just sat down behind my desk when I heard the bell out front, signaling that someone had come in. I really needed to give Gale more shifts, I thought to myself as I struggled to get up. My leg was still weak, although I worked out every day to build the strength back up.

I rounded the corner and saw Chris walking towards me.

"Hey, man, how the hell are you doing?" he greeted me, holding his hand out for one of our bro shakes.

. . .

"Good, man. How about you? Things going well?"

"Not too bad. Work's been insane. I just got off shift and thought I'd come and see you. Check out the new place now that you've settled in," he said, looking around. The entire shop still wasn't completely finished, but it was almost done.

"Well, this is it," I said, holding my arms open. The construction guys will be back to finish everything next week," I said limping, out the door to take Chris on a tour of the place.

He was quiet as he followed me into the back area where we stored our equipment. "How's the leg and back?" he questioned.

"Better, thanks." I wasn't one to complain—never had been. Life had just handed me yet another hurdle to jump over. Instead of feeling sorry for myself, which I had done plenty of when I had been in the hospital, I now looked at it as a gift.

. . .

"Good to hear, and you're going to be just fine. I've been passing out your name."

"Thanks, man. I appreciate it. So, what's up? What brings you all the way over to the other side of town?"

Chris sat down on a wooden box and crossed his arms over his chest. "It's Becca."

"Ah Becs. I haven't seen her since my coming home party. How's she doing?"

"Good, but I'm concerned. She called me over to her place last night. She's in danger. I'm feeling a little uneasy about her being on her own."

"Why? What's going on?"

. . .

"She apparently got herself mixed up with this guy. They had a falling out, and he put his fist through her kitchen wall. She apparently got out of the shower last night and found some writing on her mirror. There was no one in her apartment, but she claims that things are being moved around her office, and she feels like she might be being followed."

"Why don't you just pull him aside and deal with him?"

"That's the thing. We haven't met him."

I felt the sudden urge to want to protect Becca. She had always been rather special to me. She'd written to me while I had been on tour—a secret that we kept just between us. Her letters had kept me company on all the cold and lonely nights away from home, and I'd be lying if I said I hadn't started having feelings for her. After the injury, I fought to be myself. Even when I was in the hospital, she had religiously written to me. It was always the days I felt like giving up the most when her letters would arrive.

. . .

"What do you need from me?"

"Well, for starters, an alarm system, and anything else you might have ideas on to keep her safe."

He didn't need to say any more. I would do whatever it took to protect her. "No problem. You know I'll get you whatever you need. How about we go over and look at her place?"

"Sure thing. The other thing: I have to go out of town for a couple weeks on a work thing."

"Say no more. She can call on me."

"That's not what I was thinking," Chris said, looking at me.

"Of course, your work guys can handle it better," I said, going back to looking for a complete system to set up in her house.

"I was hoping you might stay with her while I'm gone?"

I dropped what I'd been holding and swallowed hard at his words. "Sure, I guess I could stay at her place. Or her at mine if it makes you feel any better."

"Really?"

"Yep, not a problem. We will look at her apartment first though."

"Okay. I'm gonna run home and get some rest and I'll drop by at the end of the workday."

"Sounds good. That will give me time to put some stuff together as well. See you around five?"

. . .

"I'll be here."

Chris walked out of the building, leaving me once again in the quiet. I sat down behind my desk and took a sip of my now lukewarm coffee. I had no idea what I had gotten myself into. Why had I agreed to stay with her. The longer I sat there thinking about staying with her the more I worried she would find out how I truly felt.

I shook those thoughts from my head. I wasn't there to fall in love with her or to make her fall in love with me. I was there to protect her, to do a job. I drank down the remains of my coffee and went to work figuring out what system would be best to take to Becca's.

Becca

"I still don't understand why you didn't call the landlord to change your locks. That is why you pay rent, Becca," Dad said as he stood up and turned the deadbolt a few times to make sure it was working perfectly.

"I just figured you could get it done sooner. Besides, the landlord takes forever to get things done, Dad. It took him over a month to come and clear a clogged drain, and to be honest, if it hadn't of backed up, it probably would still not be fixed," I said, leaning in and kissing him on the cheek. "Could you also put this on?" I said, handing Dad the little swing bar door lock I had purchased.

"Becca, I just installed a deadbolt. You really think you need this as well?" Dad took that package and flipped it over a couple of times in his hands.

"Dad, please, the apartment down the hall had a break-in two nights ago. Yes, it's necessary," I lied.

I hadn't told Dad the real reason I wanted the locks changed, and I hoped that Chris hadn't mentioned anything to him either. I didn't want him to worry about me. I smiled as I watched Dad crack the package open. Within five minutes, he had the additional lock on the door. He had just shut and tested the locks again when we heard voices in the hall, followed by a loud knock.

Dad pulled the door open and was greeted by Chris. "Dad, what are you doing here?" Chris asked with surprise in his voice.

"Becca's neighbor had a break-in. She wanted a new lock. Honestly, I think it's overkill, but whatever."

Chris glanced over at me with a knowing look, and I shrugged. "You know my motto, Dad: one can never be too safe." I sang, trying to keep Dad's attention focused off of Chris.

Chris let out a laugh at my response, yet I smiled at my brother, thankful that he hadn't come out and told Dad the real reason for all of this.

"Shit, kids, I've got to run," Dad said, dropping a screwdriver into his tool bag. "I'm late for a meeting with the crown. Call me later," Dad said, kissing my cheek, and then shook hands with Chris before taking off in the direction of the elevator.

"I'm glad to see you at least took my advice," Chris said as he checked out the work Dad had just completed.

"Yep, oh, and I called the phone company. They switched my phone number."

"Good. So they cooperated with you under the directions I gave you."

"Yes. There was no problem at all," I said, bending to pick up my laundry basket off the floor. I had dropped the warm clothes there when Dad had arrived, and if I didn't get them folded, they would wrinkle. "So what brings you over here on your day off?"

I finished folding the T-shirt in my hand and turned to look at my brother when my apartment door swung open and Grant walked in. He carried with him a black duffel bag, which he set on the table across from me, and nodded. I looked over to my brother and frowned. "What is going on?"

"Look, Grant is here to check things over."

"Hey, Becs," Grant said as he dropped another box of stuff on the floor, along with another duffel bag. "How you doing?" he said, coming over and pulling me in for an enormous hug.

I wrapped my arms around him, pressing my small

body into his large, muscular frame, and breathing in his musky scent. He'd always smelled good, and today was no exception. I lingered in his arms a little longer than I probably should have, and when I noticed Chris staring, I finally pulled away.

"I'm okay. You don't need to do anything though. My brother is probably overreacting. Besides, Dad changed the locks, and I have a new number," I blurted, throwing down the T-shirt I'd folded to hide my under-garments that were sitting on the top of the basket. I eyed the box and duffel bags that sat on the floor as Grant wandered over to the sliding glass doors and fiddled with the lock.

"Becca, I want to talk to you." Chris sat down on my couch and signaled for me to sit down.

"What is it?" I said, sitting across from him, worried that he may have found something out.

"Grant is going to stay with you while I'm out of town, Becca."

My eyes flew to my brother and then over to the six-foot-two hunk of muscle that stood in my living room.

"Um, no, I'm fine, Chris. Really."

"You're fine? Really, Becs? What if this guy had gotten a copy of your key and when you were at work, he came in and installed cameras and listening devices throughout this apartment?" Grant murmured while still fiddling with the lock on the door. "You still fine?" he asked, looking to me.

It took me by surprise that Grant had spoken up. In all the time I had known him, he rarely interrupted when Chris and I were talking.

"Well...um... you don't think he did that, do you?" I asked, glancing around my apartment, meeting Grants slate-grey eyes.

"Never know. I've seen it done," Chris said, getting up and grabbing an apple from the bowl on the counter.

I took a deep breath and looked around the room. I swallowed hard. "Would you two stop trying to scare me."

"He's not trying to scare you. That is why I am going to stay here until we get your stalker."

I glanced over to Chris, who kept nodding while he bit into the apple. Then I looked over to Grant, who stood staring at me. I already knew I didn't stand a chance in trying to talk either of them out of this. Even if I could, I wouldn't even know where to begin to try.

"All right, I've got to get home and get packed up for this trip," my brother said, taking the last bite of his apple and turning to give me a hug.

"Be safe," I whispered.

"You'll be fine. I feel better knowing Grant is here.

You should too," he whispered in my ear before letting me go. "Anyway, man, I'm outta here." Chris held out his hand and Grant shook it.

"No worries. I'll look after her," Grant said, shaking my brothers hand before turning his attention back to the lock.

Once I'd returned from walking Chris to the door and saying good-bye, I walked back into my living room to find Grant fishing through one bag he had brought. Then he reached into a box and pulled out a set of cameras.

"What are those for?" I questioned.

"To monitor all entrances. I will have them hooked to a hard drive to tape everything, that way everything is on film. Now, are these the only two entrances into this apartment?"

I nodded, my face heating. There was no way he was putting one of those in my bedroom.

Grant looked at me. "Becca?"

"This is it," I said, turning away from him so he couldn't see my flushed face, which I knew would give me away.

"Um, I'm sure your brother told me you had another one."

"Of course, he did," I whispered to myself and let out a huff. "It's in my bedroom. Is it really necessary to put one in there?"

I turned around and met Grant's eyes. He looked away quickly, a slight flush to his cheeks. "No, it's fine. I'll put one just outside of the bedroom door."

"Thanks."

I went back to folding the rest of the clothes in the basket as Grant made himself busy installing the first two cameras in the pathways of the doors. When I finished, I carried the basket down the hall and began putting my clothes away in my dresser. The nervousness I felt being around Grant alone was almost unbearable. I blew out a breath and did my best to calm my nerves. I had finally stopped shaking as I moved to the next drawer when Grant came into the bedroom.

"This the only other door?" he asked, again examining the lock on the sliding door?

"Yep."

It felt awkward having him in the bedroom where I slept, where I'd dreamt of him not that long ago. I had dreamed of him being in here, but not to check the locks on the sliding doors. I glanced over at him out of the corner of my eye and watched him. For whatever reason, he had never seemed interested in me, though, and always kept things on the friends level.

"Why don't you tell me about this guy?"

"What do you want to know?"

"Everything. Where you met, how long you've known him, how long you've dated him, where he lives, have you been intimate, everything," Grant said, shrugging, while looking around for the perfect spot to place the last camera.

"His name is Jace. We met at The Wine Cellar. I was there for a work event, and after everyone left, I stayed behind for a while to unwind. I sat at the bar where he was bartending. He's only been working there about six months. Anyway, we talked that night, and before I left, we had exchanged numbers. About a week later, he texted me and asked me on a date. That was about seven months ago."

"He lives here in Merlot?"

I nodded. "Yes, over off Champagne trail, number 742 Apt 4A."

"It's not the best area, Becs."

"I know. I don't ever go there. He always comes here."

"That's a good thing. Chris said he put his fist through a wall."

"Yes, he was upset because he had been after me to take him to meet the family. The weekend we were supposed to go, I ended up having to work. He got angry. That would be the best way to describe it."

"Angry because you had to work?"

"Yeah, he had been messaging me that afternoon, and I was in meeting after meeting. It really bothered him I didn't answer him. He claimed I was ignoring him."

"I see. You think that is normal behaviour?"

I shook my head and closed the dresser drawer. "I'm not making excuses, but it only happened once. Perhaps he was having a bad day." I shrugged.

"Perhaps, or perhaps he is an obsessive and controlling ass. Exactly how involved were the two of you?" He stopped what he was doing, and his eyes skimmed my body, an uncomfortable silence falling between us.

I could feel my face flush at his question. "We weren't, if that is what you are asking."

Grant smiled shyly and walked over to the bedroom doorway, looking up at the ceiling in the hallway and holding up a camera to see if he could get a good angle.

"So you are sure he doesn't have a key?"

"I'm positive. I never gave him one."

"Do you think he took anything—credit or debit cards, or even statements?"

"Why would he take those?"

"Did he ever mention things you had purchased? Things that you might not have told him?"

I shook my head. There was nothing I could remember him bringing up. "No, nothing like that."

"I want you to go over your statements and high-light anything that you don't recognize.

"I can. I just don't see what difference that is going to make."

"Just please do as I ask."

"Fine. You don't think that three cameras are overkill in a 1200 square foot apartment?"

Grant shrugged, "Maybe, but one can never be too safe Becs."

I smiled at his answer and I wanted to ask him more questions, but he busied himself hanging the last camera, and I continued with the laundry. He spent the evening on his laptop, signing into the camera's and checking the view of each of them, while I sat on the couch watching TV.

I yawned and stretched once the show I'd been watching was over and shut the TV off. "Well, I think I am off to bed. I have to work in the morning. You going to be okay out here?"

Grant looked up from the laptop and nodded. "Yep, I'll be good."

"Did you want a pillow and blankets?"

"Nah, I probably won't sleep much. If I do ,it will be from that chair right there," he said, pointing to the armchair he had moved and now sat in the corner.

"You can't possibly sleep in that chair. Let me grab you some blankets and a pillow."

"Becs, I hate to break it to you, but I have slept in way worse places than this chair. I'll be fine." I watched Grant stand and steady himself before he walked over to me. He leaned in and placed a kiss on my forehead, his lips lingering there just long enough to send a shiver down my spine. "Go get some sleep. I'll be here if you need me." He turned around and went and sat back down, paying no attention to the fact that I was still standing there watching him.

Grant

I'd pulled the blinds and shut the lights off hours ago. I sat in the armchair, behind the computer, my eyes heavy, as I struggled to stay awake. When I felt my head do another bob, I decided that perhaps I should try to sleep. I stood up and stretched, my shoulder screaming in agony. I pulled my shirt off over my head, dropping it to the floor beside my chair. I undid my belt, dropping my jeans to the floor, and I pulled the untouched duffle bag towards me and pulled out a pair of shorts, slipping them on.

Becca had been asleep for almost three hours. I sat down in the oversized armchair, my legs raised on the ottoman that sat in front of me. My leg ached, so did my head, and I reached for my bottle of medication, downing two pills.

I closed my eyes. I had finally figured out where the best placement for this chair was. It had only taken me an hour, but from where I sat, I could see from every vantage point. I could see the front entryway, the hallway, and I sat beside the sliding door in the living room. If he came in that entrance, it would be his worst mistake. There was no way he could sneak up on me.

I took another drink of water and rested my head back on the chair. My neck was also killing me. It had been a while since I had slept sitting up, and it was proving to be a little more difficult than I once remembered. I stretched, hoping to ease some tightness and pain that I was feeling, but to no avail. I was kicking myself for being so stubborn. I should have let Becca get me pillows and blankets before she had gone off to sleep.

Once I had gotten comfortable and the pain medication kicked in, I could feel myself drifting off when I heard something. I sat up and listened hard. I could hear a tiny whimper coming from her bedroom. I got up out of the chair to see that Becca was okay. Right before they discharged me from the hospital, I remembered she had mentioned she'd been having bad dreams in her letters, and I remembered wanting to comfort her. There were many things I remembered wanting to do to her from the other side of the world, yet now that she stood here in front of me, I could barely get up the courage to meet her for a lunch or dinner date.

I hobbled down the hall and stopped just outside her bedroom. She had left the door ajar, and I placed my hand on the door and carefully pushed it open. She lay in bed, wrapped in blankets, thrashing about, whimpering in her sleep. I knew all about bad dreams, and I wondered what it was she was dreaming about.

I watched her for a minute through the cracked door and was about to turn around when I heard what sounded like crying.

"Bec?" I whispered.

Another tiny whimper escaped her, and she moved her arm about, trying to send away whatever was in her dream.

"Bec?" I whispered louder this time, trying to wake her but not scare her.

"No, Jace…" she murmured and began crying again.

I pushed the door open enough to accommodate my enormous frame and walked over to the opposite side of the bed. Should I wake her? Should I leave her to fight through the demons in her dream? I didn't know. Instead, I stood there trying to decide what to do. I knew she was going to freak if I touched her. Hell she would freak if she woke up and found me standing over top of her as well. Either way she was going to freak. I took in a deep breath and kneeled on the bed.

"Becca," I said, touching her shoulder and lightly shaking her. "Wake up. You're having a bad dream."

I turned on the bedside light and was just about to turn back to face her when she surprised me by screaming. I went to grab her and was taken aback by the sharp sting of a slap across my face.

Becca was sitting up, hair all disheveled, breathing hard, staring at me with large, round eyes. Immediately, her hands went to cover her mouth.

"My God, Grant, I am so sorry. I—"

"It's all right. I deserve it. I heard you thrashing about and wanted to come and check on you. I should have probably just let you sleep, but instead I woke you. It's my fault. I deserved that."

"You scared me," Becca said, running her hand through her hair, her eyes watery with tears.

"I'm sorry," I said, rubbing my cheek.

"I was dreaming about—"

"Jace, I know. You said his name. Are you okay?"

She pulled her knees up to her chest and said nothing for a little while. She just sat there huddled in a ball, twirling her fingers in the sheets. I felt oddly out of place being in her bedroom with her, but I didn't want to move in case she wanted to talk. I watched as her eyes travelled over my bare chest before meeting my eyes.

"Could you get me some water?"

"Sure."

Within minutes, I had returned with a glass of water and set it on her bedside table. She was still in the same position she had been when I had left. I walked back around and sat down on the opposite side of the bed, this time leaning my back against the headboard.

She took a sip of water and placed the glass back down on the table. Once again, she ran her fingers through her soft-looking hair. "I can't get the nightmare out of my mind."

I knew exactly what she was talking about. I had been plagued with nightmares myself after I had returned from the Middle East. They were always the same—trapped in the MRAP, everyone dead or injured, hearing the footsteps on the gravel, waiting to die. I closed my eyes and put myself in her place. "You just need to close your eyes and breathe," I whispered, trying to calm her with the tone of my voice.

She did as I suggested and closed her eyes, trying to calm her breathing, but the longer she sat there, the more the rapid breathing returned. "I can't, Grant. I can't get that dream out of my mind. Would you do me a favour?"

"Anything," I said, my eyes closed.

"Would you stay with me until I fall asleep?" she questioned. "I just want to be held for a little while."

I looked over at her. She sat there looking straight ahead, almost as if she were afraid to look at me for fear I would say no. There was no way I would say no. Over the past few years, there had been many times I had wanted to hold her. I knew I probably shouldn't—I was here as a favor to her brother, to do a job—but she was practically begging me.

Swallowing hard, I raised my arm. "Come here.," I whispered as I shuffled my body down in the bed. In a matter of seconds, she was at my side. I had barely gotten comfortable before her head rested on my shoulder and her left leg swung over mine, causing me to jump as she hit the site I'd had surgery on.

"Oh my God, did I hurt you?"

I reached under the blankets, grabbing her leg and readjusting it. "Just my bad leg is all. A couple spots are still sensitive."

"I didn't mean to." She looked up at me with forgiveness in her eyes.

"I know you didn't mean to. It's okay now. Just relax and close your eyes," I said, holding her tightly against me, my other hand removing the hair from her face.

When I felt her breathing finally slow, I reached up and turned off the light and allowed myself to relax back in the bed. She snuggled against me, and I pulled the blankets up around her shoulders. Her hand rested on my chest, and I glanced down to see her peering up at me.

"Do you remember when we used to write back and forth?" she asked.

"Of course, I remember. Your letters got me through my years in the Middle East. They also got me through my time in the hospital too."

"Can I tell you something?"

"Of course."

She turned her eyes from me and lay there. "If I told you I used to dream of this, of you holding me like this, what would you say?"

I swallowed hard and looked down to see her peering up at me with those blue eyes of hers. I had dreamed so long of lying with her like this as well, but I never thought she felt the same. The longer I looked into those blue eyes of hers, the more I wanted her. I wanted to tell her exactly how I felt, but the words wouldn't come out. Instead, I tilted my head, leaned into her, and brushed my lips ever so gently against hers, my hand cupping her cheek.

Becca

I yawned. It was only five in the morning, and I stood in front of the bathroom mirror, wrapped in a large, plush towel. I glanced at my reflection, at the dark lines surrounding my eyes. I could hear banging as Grant moved around the living room, finishing his workout I had interrupted this morning when I came out of the bedroom. He had been down on the floor, doing crunches—one hundred to be exact—and he had barely looked in my direction when he rolled over on the floor to plank. I stumbled into the bathroom with nothing more than a murmured good morning, even though I would have preferred to watch.

I wanted to crawl back into bed and never get up again after last night. Instead, I climbed in the shower, allowing the hot water to run over me.

The heat of the water wrapped around me like a protective blanket, the same way I had felt last night with Grant's arms around me. How safe I had felt with his powerful hands roaming my body as he kissed me hard, pulling me closer to him. Instantly, I had been lost in his kiss and allowed my body to respond. *I sat up and threw my leg over his lap, straddling him, and as I lowered myself onto him, I felt his hard shaft between my legs. I ground down on him, a gruff moan escaping his lips. I went to repeat the action, and that was when he stopped kissing me. In one swift movement, he lifted me off him, got up out of the bed mumbling something about what had gone on between us was an absolute mistake, and then he slammed the bedroom door behind him, leaving me alone.*

I blinked away the water that had run into my eyes. Perhaps I was losing my touch, I thought. I felt so rejected last night, so hurt that he didn't want to be with me, but that feeling had passed and now I felt angry. I had wanted to follow him last night. Hell, I had still wanted to ask him this morning what was wrong, what I had done to make him leave, what it was about me he found so repulsive, but I didn't. Last night I sunk down under the covers and cried myself to sleep. Nothing had changed this morning either. I had run into the bathroom instead of asking him. Not only was I confused, but I was also very embarrassed.

I shut the water off and climbed out of the shower. I needed to focus. I needed to shut my mind off from all the noise that was Grant. He was here as a favor to my brother, to protect me while he was away—not for any other reason. I searched through my phone and played one of my playlists while I did my hair and makeup and put on my uniform. Then I wandered into the living room to find an array of tools and manuals sprawled out everywhere. Grant barely looked at me before he got up off the floor and made his way to the bathroom.

I ignored him and went to the kitchen where I now sat enjoying my *Cosmo* magazine with my bowl of cereal and coffee. I was in the middle of an article about the dangers of dating a friend when Grant appeared in the doorway. He leaned up against the doorframe and looked at me.

"So, we have some rules to cover," he grunted.

"Excuse me? Rules?"

"Yes, rules."

"My God, you sound just like Chris," I said, slamming my magazine down on the table and getting up to put my bowl in the sink.

"Well, you're right. I might sound like him, but to be honest, I really don't care. First rule, I will drive you to work and pick you up."

I spun around, looking at him like he was crazy.

"Why? What for? I have a perfectly fine vehicle down in the parking lot outside."

"Yes, you are right, you do. It's also a vehicle that Jace knows, so if he is following you and you have your vehicle, he will know right where you are. My vehicle, however, he does not know."

"Fine." I pouted. "Whatever you want. Have it your way," I muttered under my breath.

"Aren't you going to finish your breakfast?" he said, looking in the sink at my half-eaten cereal as he grabbed a glass from the cupboard.

I shrugged. "No, I'm not all that hungry, if you must know. Now what is next?"

"Becs you should eat."

"Yes, Dad, I know I should eat. Now what is next?" I said, getting annoyed.

"There will be no going out to lunch with the girls at work or leaving the property at work for any reason. You are never to be alone."

I chuckled. "Um, I hate to break it to you, but sometimes I have to leave the office, you know. I do a daily postal run, and sometimes I have to pick something up from a store."

"You are a manager, correct?"

I sighed. "What does my position have to do with it?"

"Becs, just answer me." He leaned up against the fridge and smirked.

"Yes, I'm a manager."

"Well, managers are supposed to delegate, aren't they? You can have an employee go." Grant shrugged.

I rolled my eyes. "What about the bathroom? Can I at least go to the bathroom on my own or do I need a supervisor for that as well?" I said, dropping another spoon of sugar into my coffee.

"Becca, this isn't funny."

"Believe me, I know it isn't funny. None of this is funny, but I didn't think you would babysit me."

"I'm not, but if I am going to do what is needed then I need to know where you are at all times. Now, if I am going to take you to work and make it to work on time myself, we need to get going."

"Fine," I bit out, reluctantly pouring my hot coffee into a travel mug and placing my favorite mug in the sink. "Aren't you going to eat anything?" I questioned as I grabbed my purse, laptop, and coat.

"I will get breakfast after I drop you off. Let's go."

Grant didn't wait. He pulled the door open and made his way down the hall. I rushed to lock my apartment door and followed him. I had just about caught up to him when my cell phone rang. I signaled to Grant to wait for a minute while I dug through my purse, but he ignored me and kept walking.

"Answer it in the car," he bit out.

"What if it's work?"

"Well, if it's work, they can wait for two minutes while you get into the car, or better yet, they can leave a message."

I clenched my jaw tightly, biting back the words I wanted to yell at him. I ran to catch up with Grant, who was now standing inside the elevator waiting impatiently for me. The ride down to the main floor of my building was quiet. He didn't look my way, he made no small talk, he kept his eyes trained ahead, and when the door opened, he bolted from the elevator.

I followed him to his truck, dumping my things on the floor in the front seat before climbing in. I had barely set my travel mug in the cup holder when he barked, "Buckle up," as he put his truck into reverse.

"God, you are so bossy," I grumbled, reaching for my belt and pulling it across my chest. I reached for my purse and quickly dug out my cell phone.

Grant didn't respond. Instead he reversed out of the parking spot and started heading to the Moscato Resort and Spa. I finally found my cell phone in the bottom of my purse and noticed I had four messages waiting for me. I quickly keyed in my code and listened.

The first was my boss letting me know of a meeting first thing this morning that I had forgotten about. Good thing I was going in early. Second was my brother reminding me to listen to Grant. I rolled my eyes and skipped the rest of his lecture. The third and fourth message started playing and chills ran down my spine. I reached over slowly and placed my hand on Grant's forearm, gripping him to get his attention.

"Becca, what is it?"

"It's..." I swallowed hard. "It's Jace. He...he left messages."

"Give it to me," Grant said, pulling over and taking my phone from me.

He sat there listening, while I sat there shaking. Jace's voice sounded crazed. In his second message, he threatened me because he knew that a man had spent the night with me. Which told me he was outside of my apartment all night, or he had some way to see.

When Grant had finished listening to the messages, he replayed them, listening to them again. Then he looked over at me and realized that I wasn't okay.

When I looked over his way, I could feel my bottom lip trembling. Grant typed something into my phone and then cleared the message from my phone and hung it up, holding it out for me to take.

"It's okay, Becca. It was only a message."

"Ha, easy for you to say. Did you hear him? He sounded crazy, Grant."

"Yes, exactly, and this is why I put those rules in place. Please, just do whatever I tell you okay?"

I sat there looking straight ahead and then turned to meet Grant's eyes. "Okay, I promise." I felt his hand on mine, and then he interwove his fingers with mine, giving my hand a gentle squeeze.

"It's going to be okay, I promise you. I will not let him hurt you."

"I know," I muttered, still not sure how safe I really felt.

Grant wasted no more time. He pulled out onto the road and continued on his way, while I slid my phone back into my purse.

We finally pulled up out front of the resort. I knew he was waiting for me to get out, but I couldn't move. I felt literally tied to the front seat.

"Becca? We are here."

"I know. It's just, what if he is in my—"

"Then you leave immediately and call security."

Grant glanced at his watch. "Becca, I am going to be late." If there was one thing I knew about Grant, he hated being late.

"What are you going to do today?"

"I have a little digging I want to do. I want to find

out as much as I can about Jace. So, if you need me, I will be available by phone. Otherwise, I will pick you up at what... four?" he said, glancing at his watch again.

"Okay, yes, four." I could barely comprehend what he was saying, I was so scared. I knew I didn't finish work until five, but at this moment, I didn't want to go in at all and just agreed with whatever it was he said.

"All right, I will see you then."

I opened the car door first, looking in the mirror to make sure no one was around, and then grabbed my bag and ran to the front of the building. I didn't bother to look back to see if Grant was sitting there waiting until he knew I was inside or if he had already pulled away. It was going to be a long day, and I couldn't wait until I was back home in my apartment.

Grant

I drove to the closest coffee shop after dropping Becca off. I pulled into the drive thru, placed my order, and now I sat here waiting. I dialed into my voicemail and listened once again to the messages I had forwarded from Becca's phone. I hoped that maybe I could hear something in the background, but there was nothing but a crazed Jace on the other end. I hung up the phone and leaned back into my seat, inching my car up to the window.

"Sir, your coffee and bagel."

I smiled. Perfect timing, I thought to myself as I reached out and took the cup and bag from her. Once everything was situated, I pulled through and headed to the office.

It had taken me a half hour to hand out the assignments. I sat in my office debating what my next move was going to be. I once again dialed into my voice mail and listened to the messages again.

Irritated, I blew out a breath. Becca had said he worked at The Wine Cellar as a bartender. I figured perhaps I'd have lunch there, that way I could scope him out. See exactly what this guy was like.

The Wine Cellar was a busy place. I pulled into the parking lot and looked for a place to park. After finding one, I went inside and was directed to the bar. I had just placed my order when one bartender asked for my drink order.

"I'll just take a soda please."

"Sure thing," she said, winking at me.

I rolled my eyes as she walked away and checked my messages.

"Here you are," she said, setting the glass down in front of me. "You new to these parts?" She crossed her arms and leaned onto the bar.

"Nope, grew up here."

"Oh, I don't think I've ever seen you before."

I said nothing regarding that. I wasn't here to make small talk or to have some chick hit on me. "Actually, I was wondering, is Jace in today. I'm an old friend and thought I'd stop in and see him."

A funny look came over her face, and she held up

her finger at me, signaling for me to hold on. I thought perhaps someone was asking for a drink, but as I watched her, she walked over and whispered something to another staff member, then they both turned and looked my way.

A couple of minutes later, she disappeared and the woman she had told approached me. "Can I help you with something?" she asked.

"Yeah, I am an old friend of Jace, and I thought I'd come by and see him. I was wondering if he was working today?"

"I'm sorry, but Jace no longer works here."

"Oh. That's odd. I was just speaking to him the other day."

"Jace was fired a week ago."

"Oh." I frowned. "He was the one who told me to stop by. Mind me asking you what happened?"

"I shouldn't tell you, but you look trustworthy enough. He'd come into work fine, but as his shift went on, he appeared to get highly agitated. He'd be on the phone, sneaking away to make calls while working the bar, and leave in the middle of his shifts. I can't have that. As you can see the place is packed."

I nodded in understanding. "I'm sorry if I upset the young lady," I said.

"It's all right. She will be fine. Most of the female staff

here were the ones who reported him. He didn't take to kindly to any of them. He was terrible at managing his anger as well. Some of them felt his wrath."

It was then that the young lady returned with my burger and fries, setting the plate down in front of me. "Thank you," I mumbled.

"Well, enjoy your lunch."

Both women walked away to leave me in peace while I at;, only I wasn't in peace. The thought of this lunatic now running around gave me new cause to worry. At least before, if I knew he was here, we knew where he was. Now I didn't have a damn clue.

The second I finished eating, I paid my bill and headed out to my car. I started the engine and sat there with my hands on the wheel. The next stop would be his apartment over on Champagne Trail.

I looked around at the buildings as I pulled into the rundown area. I drove halfway down the road and parked the car out front of the address Becca had given me. I glanced up and saw a "for rent" sign on one of the front windows. Perfect, I thought to myself as I cut the engine. I now had an excuse why I was here, I thought as I climbed out of my truck and walked towards the front of the building where two men sat out front. They both eyed me as I approached the front of the building.

It was no secret I didn't belong here, but I needed to play it up.

"Hey, friend, how can we help you?" one guy who sat on the steps asked as he stood up.

"I'm here to see about the apartment for rent."

"For that, you'd need Jimmy." The other one shrugged.

"Is Jimmy here?"

"Nope, he's never around 'cept to collect the monthly rent."

"I see."

"It's a nice place, though. The one that's for rent. We can't believe the guy who had it gave it up. Two bedrooms for only fifty dollars more than what I pay a month."

I nodded, half listening to what they were saying.

"Maybe we should see if we can swap it," the other said.

"Still can't believe that dumbass Jace would just walk away from the place. Although he wasn't very bright."

I turned my head abruptly towards them. "What did you say?"

"Meh, the guy who had it before just up and gave notice. Pissed Jimmy right off. Rumor has it he decided a day before the rent was due that he would give his thirty days. He stiffed him."

Becca had gotten tied up with a real winner, I thought to myself as I turned to head back towards my car.

"Should we tell Jimmy that you were here?"

"Nah, I'll call and book an appointment," I called out behind me.

"Good luck with that," they both yelled out in unison as I climbed into the front seat of my car.

I started the engine. Jace no longer had a job or a place to live. This was a worse situation than I originally thought. He was a total wild card and could be anywhere.

I pulled away from the curb and headed over to the Moscato Resort and Spa. On my way, I stopped and grabbed a coffee, and once in the parking lot, I cut the engine, sat back, and took a sip. I glanced at the clock. I was a little over an hour early to pick her up. I took another sip of my coffee and closed my eyes, putting out of my mind all the information I had found out and began thinking about last night. I'd fucked up my chances of anything with her, all because I had panicked at my body's rapid response to her.

It had been a while since I'd been with a woman, but last night had felt different from the last time. Over the years, I'd gotten to know Becca pretty well in the letters we'd exchanged. She had kept my mind occupied on the many lonely nights I'd spent overseas, and I really thought little of it at the time, but I had spent so many nights thinking about what she was doing on the other side of the world. I knew that now wasn't really the time for me to let my guard down when it came to her either; that would only distract me from what I was doing, and that was protecting her.

Yet, as I sat here, I could feel my cock stirring behind my zipper as I thought about that kiss. The way her soft lips felt against mine, the way she nipped my bottom lip between hers. When she'd straddled my lap and I felt the heat between her legs against me...I jumped at the sound of my phone ringing.

I pulled my cell phone from the holder and saw Chris's number displayed across the screen.

"Hey, man, how is it going? All okay?" he asked.

"Well, it would be if I knew where this fucker was," I barked into the phone.

"What do you mean?"

"Well, last night I started asking Becca about him. She divulged where they met and his address, so today I did a little detective work."

"And?"

"Well, interestingly enough, he no longer works at

The Wine Cellar. They fired him about a week ago. Apparently, he would grow agitated during shifts, sneaking off to make calls, and he would just disappear mid-shift. So once I discovered that, I paid a visit to his residence. You know, I just wanted to get a good look at this guy, know what I was up against."

"What did you find out?"

"His place is for rent."

"How did you find that out?"

"Ah, it was easy. Two guys who were out front of the apartment just sang like jaybirds. I didn't even need to ask them questions. They volunteered everything."

Chris let out a laugh. "Fuck, I love guys like that. Makes everything so much easier when you don't have to work for the information."

"Sure does. I didn't even need to think."

"Okay, so what is the plan?"

"Well, I'm working on that now. I'm waiting outside of Becca's work. I'll stop by the shop afterward with her to close up, then we will head back to her place and I will work it all out."

"Okay, well, keep me posted. I should be home tomorrow night at some point."

"Sounds good."

I hung up and sat back and thought hard about what to do next. I needed to find this guy, so I could at least have a location on him. I'd also need to tell Becca that I had no clue where he was. I wasn't looking forward to that conversation. I'd seen the look in her eyes this morning as she listened to the messages he had left. I'd also wanted to be the one who held her and assured her it would be okay. Worst was I knew that this guy was a ticking time bomb, and it would only be a matter of time before he exploded.

Becca

Grant had suggested dinner at The Vineyard Bar and Grill after he closed up the shop. We now sat across from one another studying the menu. The server approached the table and set a glass of white wine in front of me and an ice-cold beer in front of Grant.

"Are you ready to order yet?" she asked, pulling a pad of paper and pen from her apron pocket.

I glanced over at Grant, who still had his face in the menu and was clearly ignoring the fact that the woman had even spoken.

I looked up and smiled. "I'm sorry, but could we have a couple more minutes, please?"

The server was clearly annoyed and shoved the paper and pen back in her apron pocket, turned, and walked away.

I closed my menu and laid it in front of me. Then I looked over to Grant, who appeared to be on edge.

"Is everything okay?"

"Sorry, everything just looks good, and I am starving, which is making it hard to choose," he said, not lifting his eyes from the menu.

"It's okay."

I picked up my glass of wine and took a long sip, then pulled my phone from my pocket, clearing any emails I had already dealt with. I kept looking up at Grant, who sat there with his brow furrowed, still apparently debating on what he wanted for dinner. I knew that there was something else on Grant's mind other than hunger. He had been quiet the entire way to the shop and all the way to the restaurant. I didn't know if it had something to do with what had happened between us last night or if he had found something out today about Jace. Regardless, I planned to find out what it was.

After another few long minutes, he closed the menu with force and set it down on the table, picking up his beer and taking a swig, directing his attention to the hockey game that was playing on the screen behind the bar, once again ignoring me.

"Did you decide?"

"Yep, think I'll have the chicken."

"You think?" I let out a laugh. "You've been studying that menu for almost twenty minutes."

He shrugged. "Still undecided. Between that and the burger."

I nodded and took a sip of my wine. The server had come back, and once our order had gone in and they had delivered another round of drinks, I sat there looking out the window as Grant continued to watch the game. He had barely looked at me since he had picked me up.

A few more sips of wine mixed with an empty stomach, and I suddenly had an insurmountable amount of courage. I put my glass down, crossed my arms in front of me, leaned forward and looked directly at him.

"It's last night, isn't it?" I choked out.

"Huh? What? What's last night?"

"Grant, please stop. You've barely looked in my direction, and you haven't said much more than two words to me since you picked me up."

He blew out a breath. "Becca, I have said more than two words to you."

"Barely, and I could cut the tension between us with this butter knife," I said, holding up the knife at the side of my plate. "What is wrong? Are you mad about what happened last night?"

"Mad?"

"Yes, mad. Mad that we kissed, because I don't think I have ever had a man run out of my room that fast before in my life. I thought..."

"You thought what?"

"I thought that... Never mind, it's stupid." I decided to shut my mouth. After all, it was the alcohol talking, and I knew it. I turned my attention to a table full of kids across from us. Grant was silent for what felt like an eternity. Perhaps I had divulged too much to him when I had told him I had dreamt of him holding me the way he was. Perhaps I had bared too much of myself in that moment, and it had freaked him out to know I had thought of him that way. We had exchanged a few letters, and so what if I knew some of his deepest darkest thoughts and secrets and he knew mine? It still meant nothing. I swallowed hard, waiting for him to speak.

"Look, it wasn't you okay? It was me."

I rolled my eyes, but I felt the anger boiling inside of me. "Please spare me." I picked up my glass and downed the remainder of the wine, looking around for the server.

"I..."

I held my hand up to stop Grant from saying any more.

"Just save the old 'it isn't you, it's me' routine. I've

heard this before, believe me. You know, over the years, all those letters, perhaps I let my guard down when I admitted to you I dreamt of you holding me…I feel as if I made a fool of myself."

He picked up his beer, taking another swig, a cocky smile on his face.

"Perhaps you think that is what is bothering me, when really, it appears to be bothering you much more. I was being serious, Becca. It wasn't you."

"Then what was it?"

I was ready for some half-assed excuse and I sat there quite sure of myself that he was going to be just like the other men who had given me the 'it isn't you, it's me' speech.

"What was it?" Grant chuckled in the same manner he always had when he was put on the spot in an uncomfortable situation with his friends. "Perhaps, Becca, I didn't want to take advantage of a situation where you were feeling vulnerable in the moment. Did you ever think of that?"

Grant's words had stopped me in my tracks, and I sat there stunned for a moment. He didn't want to take advantage of a situation where I was feeling vulnerable?

"So if you are wondering why I ran out of your room, it wasn't because of you. It was because I didn't want you to think of me as some asshole who would use the fact that you were upset and scared as a simple way to get into your pants."

I frowned. I literally had no words, and then the server showed up carrying our food. She placed the plates in front of us and scurried off in another direction when she sensed the tension between us. Instead of digging into his food, Grant got up from the table and, without another word, headed towards the bathroom. I frowned. Perhaps Grant was right. Perhaps the fact that he had left the bedroom the way he had was really bothering me more than I had let on. I had no idea that he had felt that way.

Minutes later, he returned, slid into the seat across from me, and dug into his dinner, not saying another word. We ate in silence, and when it came time to take care of the bill I had offered to pay, but he wouldn't hear of it.

Once again, neither of us said anything on the drive back to my apartment. Once we got inside, I left Grant in the living room and took off into my bedroom. I needed to unwind; the tension was piling into my neck and shoulders. I grabbed my sweats and a towel and went to the bathroom where I filled the tub with hot water and a splash of bubble bath. The smell of lavender quickly filled the room, and I sank into the steaming water, leaning back and placing a hot towel over my eyes.

I listened to the silence for a while and then popped my earphones in and played my relaxing sounds play list. When the water started getting cold, I got out and dried off. I planned to make a cup of chamomile tea and head back to my room and watch a little TV. I wanted to be alone. However, when I entered the living room, I found Grant was pacing back and forth, looking rather agitated, which was odd because Grant hardly ever showed his agitation.

"Is something wrong?" I asked.

"We need to talk," he said, gesturing for me to sit down.

I did as he asked, parking myself on the couch and waiting while he continued to pace back and forth.

"What is it?"

"Look, I didn't want to tell you, but today I did some digging around on Jace."

"Oh?"

"Becs, I went to The Wine Cellar to scope him out. I just wanted to get a look at him, know what I was up against. When I asked about him, they informed me they had fired him."

A chill ran through me at that news. "Fired?"

"Yep, the manager there told me he'd been getting

distracted, was always on his phone, had bad mood swings, and would leave all hours of his shift."

I sat there not knowing what to say.

"I then went to his place over off Champaign Trail."

"And?"

"He no longer lives there. The apartment is for rent and is apparently vacant and has been since the start of the month. Which means..."

"You don't know where he is," I finished, looking around my apartment. I brought my hands up and rubbed my arms, another chill running through me.

"Correct."

"So he could be anywhere? He could be outside right now watching us."

"He could be. I doubt it, but he could be."

"My God...why did I ever..." I had to stop. My throat was getting tighter and I could feel the burn in my eyes from tears that had yet to fall. The fear that was rising in me was overwhelming.

I got up from the couch and walked over to the window, peaking out at the street below. "What am I going to do? Why did I ever agree to go out with him? Why didn't I tell Chris sooner that this had—"

I could feel myself shake as I continued peering through the blinds. I could feel the breakdown about to happen when I felt Grant's muscular hands on my upper arms. He gently pulled me back from the window and turned me around, looking down into my face.

"Becca, it's going to be all right."

"How can you say that? How can you stand there and say it will be all right when you have no clue where he is?"

"Because you are safe with me right now. I promised you that I won't let anything happen to you."

"What, are you planning to move in here? Because honestly, I don't want to be alone ever again."

I pulled away from him and headed to the kitchen. I pulled the refrigerator door open and grabbed a bottle of wine. I reached for a glass and filled it, turning to Grant. "Want one?"

He shook his head and watched as I put the bottle back and took a long drink of the cool liquid.

"What the hell was I thinking?" I asked myself out loud. "Why did I ever get involved with him? I should have known better. He was so pushy and clingy and..."

The second those words escaped my mouth, the tears poured. I stood there, crying into my glass of wine so hard I shook.

I was crying so hard I didn't notice Grant had stepped behind me and took the wineglass from my hand until I felt his hands on me again. He turned me around and placed his thumb under my chin, tipping my head up so he could look into my eyes. He took his thumb and wiped the tears from my cheeks, and I took in a deep breath, trying hard to calm down.

"Becca, listen to me. You are stronger than this. You are tougher than this."

I shook my head, not believing what he was saying, but he stopped me, placing his warm hands on my cheeks. I stopped crying and looked deep into his eyes. A calmness settled over me the longer I stared into his eyes. Slowly, he bent down and brought his lips to mine; only this time the kiss was far different from last night.

When he pulled away, I looked up at him. "I thought you didn't want to take advantage of a situation where I was vulnerable," I whispered, forgetting about everything I had learned only minutes before.

There was no response. Grant stepped forward, pressing his body into mine. My back hit the counter and he bent down and kissed me again, deeper, harder this time. I felt a surge of electricity race through my body as his hands gently gripped my hips, drawing me closer to him.

I rested my arms on his shoulders, and when our lips parted, he brought one hand up and placed it on my cheek.

"I don't, and I hope you don't think that's what I am

trying to do. Truth be told, I have wanted you since the minute I walked through the door and saw you. I wanted you the moment that first letter arrived across my path when I was deployed. What I told you tonight at dinner was the partial truth, but this is the real reason I ran: because the want I feel for you is so strong it scares even me."

Before I could say anything, his lips met mine again, his tongue parting my lips and washing through my mouth. He gripped my hips, picking me up. He placed his hands under my ass as my legs wrapped around his hips. I pulled at my shirt, quickly pulling it over my head, and crashed into his lips again as he carried me down the hall.

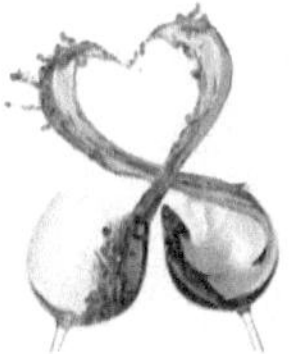

I slowly opened my eyes. I could see the start of light peering through the blinds of my bedroom, my head resting on Grant's shoulder. He was still sound asleep. I lifted my head to glance at the clock; it was only five. I put my head back down and snuggled into him, closing my eyes. I had just gotten comfortable when I felt his arms tighten around me. "Good morning," he muttered, kissing my forehead.

"Morning," I said groggily, wrapping my arms around him.

It had been a long time since I had slept as soundly as I had, but after the workout he had given me, I wasn't surprised. Being held in his arms wasn't like anything else I'd experienced, and it felt amazing to be so at ease. He held me for a bit and then stretched. "I should get showered," he said, sitting up and throwing the covers off his naked body.

I couldn't help but allow my eyes to wash over his strong and scarred body. Each wound told a story, and I wanted to hear about them all. He leaned back down and placed a long kiss on my lips and made his way to the bedroom door.

"I'll get the coffee on."

I wandered into the kitchen and busied myself. Once I finished, I looked around. I was feeling rather anxious now, knowing that I had to go into work today. I saw the mail sitting on the table where I had left it and flipped through the stack of bills I still hadn't opened. When I came to the credit card statement, Grant's words rang through my mind. *"Check your statements, make sure you recognize all the transactions."*

Once we'd eaten breakfast and I'd showered, Grant

said he had a couple of calls to make before we left. I sat down with the highlighter and start going through this month's statement, highlighting every transaction I recognized.

I frowned when I got to the second page. There was a transaction I knew I hadn't made. I grabbed the red pen sitting on the table and drew a circle around the charge and put a large question mark beside it. Then I moved onto the next one. That, too, had the same charge on it. I was just about to call Grant when he came around the corner with an intense look on his face.

"Becca, we have to get a move on. I have a problem. One guy called in sick, which means a bunch of installations won't get done this morning, unless I rearrange some things before the guys get there. I need to get to the office to sort it out. I have to drop you off early."

"No problem."

I dropped the highlighter on the table and grabbed my things. I made a mental note to make sure that I remembered to tell Grant about the charges I'd found later this morning.

Grant

After dropping Becca off, I got to the office in record time. I greeted Gale, my office clerk, at the front desk and saw the relief on her face as I took the pile of installation orders for the day with me.

"I'm so sorry to call you so early this morning, Grant. I just didn't know how you wanted me to handle this," she said, following me with another pile of work orders.

"No worries, Gale. I think I should be able to get it figured out before the guys get here so we don't miss anyone. I will let you know if I need you to call any of the clients to reschedule."

"Thanks, Grant. I feel just horrible."

"No worries, Gale. It's not a big deal, honestly."

She nodded. "How about I get you a cup of coffee."

"That would be great, thanks." I couldn't get mad at her. She was new to the city and closer to my mother's age. Despite having tried to show her around our area, she still didn't know it well.

I walked into my office and started sorting through the day's assignments, quickly tacking an installation onto anyone who was lighter than normal and close to the area. I had just finished as, one by one, the installation guys appeared at my door and stepped into my office to grab their day's assignments.

Once everyone was on the road, I picked up the lukewarm coffee that Gale had dropped on my desk and took a sip. I had just sat down behind my desk when Gale appeared at my door.

"Grant, I forgot to tell you, I received a call from a customer yesterday afternoon once you'd left for the day. You installed a system in his storage locker a few weeks back. He asked that you disconnect them today."

"What, like stop the feed?"

"Yeah. He says he knows he paid for the entire year, but he asked that you disconnect them for this week only and start them again next Sunday."

I frowned at the strange request when my phone vibrated, and I peered down to see Becca's name flash across the screen.

"I'm sorry, Gale, I have to take this," I said, reaching for the phone.

"Grant, he asked that they be disconnected yesterday."

"Yep, no worries. I will get to it right after this call."

I spun around in my chair and picked up the phone, thoughts of last night running through my mind. "Hey, you, miss me already?" I chuckled into the phone.

"Grant."

I could hear the fear in her voice as she said my name, and alarm rose in my chest. "Becs, what's wrong?"

"We are being evacuated. There's been a bomb threat." Becca's voice was shaky, and I imagined she was on the verge of tears. She seemed to be out of breath as well.

"What? Where are you?" I said, spinning around in my chair, feeling around on my desk for my keys.

"I'm heading down the back staircase of the resort, toward the back entrance to the rear parking lot."

"All right, listen to me. Keep calm and just breathe. As soon as you are outside, you head over to the Wine Glass Fountain."

"Grant, I'm scared. I have a bad feeling about this."

"Becca, listen, it's going to be fine, I will meet you there in twenty minutes. Whatever you do, don't go anywhere else, or with anyone else. Tell your boss that that is where you will be. I will be there as quick as I can," I barked, getting up as quickly as I could without my leg giving out under my weight.

"Okay. Please hurry, Grant."

I could hear the fear in her voice and wanted nothing more than to be with her and comfort her. "I'm on my way, Becs." I hung up and grabbed my jacket and keys and headed out the front door, yelling back to Gale that I would be back. Once in my truck, I dialed Chris. I figured if this was a bomb threat, he was probably already on his way there.

"Chris here," he barked into the phone. I could hear multiple voices in the background.

"Hey! You hear about the bomb threat over at the Moscato?"

"Yep, I just got back, and we are on our way now. Is Becca with you?"

"I dropped her off at work this morning. She's already called me, and I'm on my way to meet her at the wine glass fountain."

"Okay, we just arrived. I've got to go."

The phone went dead, and I turned the corner and jammed on my breaks. There were people everywhere, lining the middle of the street, making it impossible for me to pass. I pulled over and parked the truck, quickly scanning the crowd of people for any sign of Becca. I could see the fountain from where I parked, and I pushed my way through the crowd, making my way over to the base of the fountain, looking in every direction for her.

When I didn't see her immediately, I pulled my phone from my back pocket and quickly texted her. Still searching through the crowds looking for her, I held onto my phone, waiting for a response from her.

When I got to the base of the fountain, I once again searched the crowds, but still couldn't find her. Then I remembered she had said she was going out the back door of the resort. Perhaps the police had refused to let them leave the area and she was still back there. I crossed the street and got around to the back of the building, but when I got there, the police quickly escorted me away, telling me that they had evacuated all persons and that they allowed no one in the immediate area.

I could feel my frustration peak, which was odd for me after all my training, but I couldn't help it. I had to find her. I combed through the crowds for over an hour with no luck. I was out of my mind, and I now stood out front of the resort, watching as police walked out, and then I spotted Chris. As soon as he saw me, he waved, signaling for me to come over.

"You find her?"

I shook my head. "No, she is nowhere. It's like she disappeared."

"All right, once my captain clears the place and they allow people to go in, I am going to get in touch with the general manager. If she isn't with them, then we are going to need the security tapes."

Two hours later, all employees had been accounted for, except Becca. We sat in the general manager's office, watching the security footage of each entrance. We finally got to the last tape and, sure enough, we saw her walk out the side door.

"Do you have the tapes from outside this entrance?" Chris questioned.

"Of course, sir." The manager shuffled through the tapes, finally finding the one we wanted to see.

We watched as Becca stepped out that back door, ran her fingers through her hair, and turned her attention to another staff member who appeared to need help. She was just about to grab hold of her when someone came up behind Becca and grabbed her, throwing a shirt over her head. We watched the entire tape, watched as Becca struggled and was thrown against the front of a white van by a man with a balaclava over his head. Then he hoisted a fighting Becca over his shoulder and threw her into the side door of the white van. We then watched as the man climbed into the front seat and reversed, making sure the van never crossed in front of the camera.

"How is it, in all this chaos, with people every-where, that no one helped her?" I blurted out.

Chris held his hand out. "Do you have any other tapes that cover the back parking lot?" Chris questioned, rewinding the tape, hoping for a hint at something, anything, that might put a mark on the vehicle, but there was none.

"No, sir, the camera for that part of the building was damaged seven months ago in an electrical storm," the manager commented, looking uncomfortable.

"What? You mean you haven't fixed it?" Chris said, getting up and leaning across the manager's desk until he was in his face.

Chris's supervisor watched and then cleared his throat, grabbing him by the shoulder and pulling him back. "All right, so they took her. Grant, we can take it from here. Sir, we are going to need that tape, and we want to speak with every employee who exited the building through that entrance. Surely, someone saw something," he said to the general manager. Within seconds, the manager had put the tape in his.

"So what's next?" I asked.

"We will get to the bottom of it, Grant. You head

home," the supervisor said, taking the tape from the manager. "Chris let's get going. You're off the case as well. It's too close to you, but do you have any clue who may have taken her, a lead we could go on?"

Chris spoke to his captain and then stayed behind with me. Grant and I looked to one another as the others left the room, tape in hand. "Grant, I know you're not going to listen, but when you get back to the apartment, if you notice anything, call me right away."

"You heard your captain. You're not supposed to be working on it either."

Chris chuckled and looked at me with a serious face. "Are you telling me you're going to sit idly by and wait?"

I looked around the room, trying to ignore his question. "Yeah, I didn't think so," Chris mumbled and left the room, leaving me standing there, alone.

I needed to find her. I had promised her I wouldn't let anything happen to her, and I had broken that promise. I rushed out the door and got into my truck, speeding across the city to her apartment.

I had been back at her apartment for a little over an hour, doing my best to recall all that she had told me. I had looked through everything, trying to find anything that may help us find her, but I came up with nothing.

I walked into the kitchen and opened the fridge,

grabbing a bottle of water. I leaned against the counter, cracked it open, and took a drink. Then I glanced down at the table. A mass of credit card statements lay in a pile on the table.

I walked over and picked the top one up, noticing a red circle on the one charge, and beside that a large question mark. I frowned and picked up the next statement and looked at the charge. Nixon's Storage for seventy-five dollars was circled on multiple statements. I grabbed the other statements that lay underneath and saw the same charge on the past seven statements. I recognized the name from somewhere, and I pulled my phone from my pocket, doing a quick search for Nixon's Storage.

My heart was immediately in my throat. I was sure it was the same storage facility I had been at a month earlier on the outskirts of Merlot. I quickly dialed the number and waited while it rang.

"Nixon's storage," a said.

"Hi, I am wondering if you can tell me if there a storage unit registered to the name of Becca Scott or a Jace Taylor?"

"I'm sorry, unfortunately, due to client confidentiality, I cannot give out that information."

Irritated, I hung up the phone and made a tight fist. Then I thought back to the strange encounter I'd had there. There had been something about the guy I'd dealt with that hadn't sat right.

Deliberating no more, I immediately dialed Chris's number and told him what I'd found and asked him to meet me over at the shop.

Becca

My head pounded as I struggled to open my eyes. I had no idea where I was; everything was dark. I tried to move my arm to wipe at my eyes. Immediately, I felt something bite into my wrists, stopping me from trying to move my arm. A loud bang came from somewhere close by. I froze and listened hard. I heard someone swear under their breath.

Panic really set in. I struggled to try to bring my arms around, but again, something dug into my wrists sharply, causing me to cry a little. They were tied together. I tried to move my feet, but the same thing happened as something sharp seared its way into my skin around my ankles.

Another loud bang caused me to jump. I lay there breathing hard, doing my best not to panic, when I felt someone put their hands on my ankles and pull me roughly into a sitting position. Instantly, I felt pain shooting up my back, and I got dizzy. I could feel myself falling backwards, but instead of letting me fall, I felt someone grab my arm, holding me up. The bright light ripped through my eyes as they ripped the blindfold away. I closed my eyes tightly as a sharp pain ran through my head.

"Open your eyes," the deep voice drawled.

I tried again to allow my eyes to adjust, finally doing my best to blink a little, but I could barely see. I blinked once, twice, and then a dark silhouette of a man stood in my view. I couldn't make out who it was as my eyes still hadn't adjusted yet. I kept blinking, finally realizing that at the moment he was paying no attention to me. He disappeared only to reappear once again, carrying something that he sat down on a wooden table. I blinked hard, my vision returning more to normal, and I looked around. I recognized nothing and had no idea where I was. I once again struggled to move but couldn't. The anxiety building in my chest was unbearable, and I could hardly breathe. I tried to swallow, but my mouth was dry, and then I realized that not only did I have tape over my mouth, but someone had shoved something in it—a rag perhaps. Once again, I tried to pull my hands to the front to rip the tape off so I could scream, but again something bit sharply into my wrists, this time causing my eyes to water.

I rested against a wall, looking around, and I realized I was sitting in the back of some vehicle. Another loud bang came from somewhere out of my line of view, and then the same man stepped into view and attached a wire to something.

The man turned and looked my way. His face was covered with a balaclava. My heart rate increased as he took a couple of steps towards me and picked me up as if I were nothing, flinging me over his shoulder. The pain in my head and back made the room spin, and I had to close my eyes to keep from throwing up. I was roughly thrown down into a chair and faced a tall man. He said nothing, just walked across the room to a bench and stood with his back to me.

I swallowed hard; my throat was now so dry it hurt. I tried to remember how I had gotten here. I remembered the bomb threat being forced to leave my office, people running in every direction when one of my coworkers grabbed me and led me towards the stairwell. I remembered calling Grant and falling behind everyone else. *Oh my God, I was supposed to meet Grant.* I imagined him waiting for me, panicking when I didn't show up. Then I remembered being grabbed me from behind as I opened the door to the back parking lot, and everything went black. An arm around my neck and a sharp blow to the head was the last thing I remembered.

I looked over at the tall, masked man and watched as he turned slowly to face me. He stood there for a moment, his eyes running over me, and then he took a step forward.

"So, you're finally awake. I didn't even hit you that hard," he said, running his forefinger down my cheek.

Chills ran through my body. I knew that voice anywhere. He stepped forward and roughly ripped the tape off my face, pulling the rag that had been shoved into my mouth with it. A large gasp of air caused me to cough. I tried to speak, but my throat was so dry it only made me cough more.

He stood there, towering over me, laughing.

"Jace?" my hoarse voice finally rang out.

"Who the fuck you think it is?" he said, pulling the balaclava over his head.

I glanced around the room. It had no windows but was full of boxes and furniture. A white, windowless van sat parked across from me, the back door open. I looked to the large metal roller door, and a chill ran through me. "Where are we?"

"Never mind where we are."

Fear ran through me and I looked around, noticing a camera up in the room's corner we were in.

He pulled a chair around and straddled it, sitting down in front of me. He studied me for a moment before he followed my line of view up to the camera. He turned and looked back at me, laughing. "Oh, princess, you think I am that stupid? Those have been deactivated. Your boyfriend won't be able to come and save you." He chuckled.

Alarm bells rang out in my head. Did he know Grant?

"What...what do you want?"

"You, you're what I want, but not in the way you might think." A slow smile spread across his lips, and I saw a glimmer in his eye I wished I hadn't seen.

"What?" I couldn't help but let out a sob. His words only made me cry more.

"Stop your crying, you cheating bitch." He stood up and paced in front of me for a couple of seconds before sitting back down.

"What are you going to do to me?"

"What are you going to do to me?" he mocked, then turned around and paced in front of me for a couple of seconds then turned back to me. "Well, after I have my way with you, which I will have, by the way, I'm going to kill you. I want your brother to suffer. To suffer the way I did when he killed my brother."

"No, no, no," I said, shaking my head, my eyes filling with tears.

Jace stood up and threw the chair he'd been sitting on across the room, the sound of it smashing into a pile of stuff causing me to jump. "ENOUGH!" he screamed, walking to me and picking me up, throwing me over his shoulder.

I felt myself go flying, and then I landed on my back onto something soft. I looked around through teary eyes and noticed I was on a bed. I looked to where he was standing near a makeshift table. He picked up a knife and a roll of duct tape and held it up for me to see.

He walked over to me and knelt onto the bed.

"No, please, Jace, get away from me," I cried, doing my best to squirm away from him. "I'll do whatever you want," I begged.

"I'll do whatever you want," he mocked again. "Do you have any idea how long I've waited for those words to come out of your filthy little mouth?"

I used my legs to squirm my way up to the top of the mattress away from him, but one hand on my leg and a rough tug and he had pulled me back down to him.

"Please, we can talk this through," I begged.

"Becca, enough. It's too late. I gave you the chance many times to do as I wanted. It was impossible, and you left me no choice. Now shut up."

I let out a cry for help, screaming at the top of my lungs. My throat felt like it was on fire.

He pulled a piece of tape from the roll quickly, and without another word, placed it over my mouth, muffling my cries for help. He then picked up the knife and held it up against my cheek, slowly pushing the cold steel against my hot skin.

"No one is here. No one is coming or you. You get that. All your brother is going to find is his sister's mangled body, that is it."

I froze as the tears poured. My chest burned from trying to suck in air that wasn't there. He placed his hand on my shoulder, holding me on my back, and I felt his hand at the waist of my jeans. He flicked the button open with his fingers, and then he took the knife and cut the zip tie from around my ankles.

I pulled out front of my shop and checked my phone for a message from Chris, but there was nothing yet. I climbed out of the truck and walked over to the front door, inserting the key into the lock.

Screeching tires caught my attention, and I turned to see Chris pull his truck into a parking space behind mine and jump out of his truck. "Hey, man, what did you find out?" he yelled as he came running toward the front door.

I held up the credit card statements and pulled the door open. "You need to look at these," I said as I rushed into my office as fast as I could and handed the bills to Chris for him to look at while I shuffled through the invoices on my desk.

"What is this?" he asked, staring down at the red

circles and question marks that stood out on the pages he held in his hand.

"I asked her to go through her credit card statements and circle anything she didn't recognize. FUCK!" I shouted as I slammed the pile of invoices I had been going through onto my desk.

"Okay, so did he steal her card?"

"I think so. I called Nixon's Storage. They wouldn't give me any information, but I also know the name of the place. I am sure I did an install there a few weeks back, in one of the lockers."

Chris looked at me as if I had lost my mind. I glanced around my office and saw another stack of invoices sitting on top of the filing cabinet. I reached for it and began sorting through the papers again. "I really need to get these files in order," I mumbled.

"So why don't we go check the place out? It's just on the outskirts of Merlot."

A surge of adrenaline rushed through me as I stared down at the invoice halfway through the pile. There it was. I had been there. I handed Chris the invoice, and then a note on my desk caught my eye: disconnect Nixon Locker Cam.

"You installed a camera inside of a storage locker?" he questioned, looking at the invoice.

I heard Chris, but all I could do was stare down at

the note that sat on my desk. I could remember Gale standing in my doorway talking to me about it when Becca had called. I had rushed to her and forgot to disconnect the feed.

"Grant? Did you hear me? Who the hell would want to pay for a monitoring feed inside of a locked storage locker?"

I pushed past Chris on my way back to my monitoring room, ignoring his question. Would this guy really be this stupid?

"Grant, would you please tell me what the fuck is going on?"

I flipped the monitor on and cycled through the feeds, my heart pounding as I came to the one I was looking for.

"Grant, please, we are wasting time here."

I looked over at Chris and pointed to the monitor. There in front of me, on the screen, was Becca. I couldn't say anything. All I could do was point to the monitor as I watched some guy kneel between her legs and hold a knife up to her cheek as she cried. A surge of anger rushed through me. I wanted to tear the guy limb from limb, and I worked hard to calm my anger.

"Holy fuck," Chris whispered under his breath as he stood watching with me. "We've got to go."

Chris tore his cell phone from his back pocket and

dialed as he ran out of the room. I could hear him talking but couldn't move from where I stood. Every nerve in my body was on fire as I stood watching the screen. Watching as the girl I had loved my entire life lay on a bed crying, scared to death. Her captor moved out of sight, moments later back into sight on the screen. He knelt on the bed, gripping her by the legs, pulling her closer to him. I flipped the feed to see what the rest of the room looked like. I studied the items on the table, and that was when I noticed a makeshift bomb.

"Grant, let's go. My boss is going to meet us there," Chris called.

It was all I could do to tear myself away from the monitor and headed out the door.

"Police are on their way."

"We have to hurry. There is a bomb," I gritted.

I rushed out the door, locking it behind me, and ran to my truck.

We pulled into the parking lot of Nixon's Storage. Emergency vehicles were everywhere, and we approached the officers at their command post.

"What do we know?" Chris's boss asked.

"She's in there. There is a bomb just inside the door on a table. It's a homemade job. I used to deal with these all the time when I was overseas. They are pretty easy to dismantle," I said, fighting my urge to run in there and save her.

"Grant, calm down. You aren't going in there," The captain said, holding his hands up to calm me.

"Do we know whose locker it is?" Chris asked, crossing his arms across his chest.

"Belongs to a Jace Taylor, known alias for Steve Mann," the sergeant answered, looking directly at Chris, giving him a knowing look.

I glanced in Chris's direction, his face going pale at the mention of the name. Chris said nothing. He just stood there staring back at his sergeant.

"Chris, you care to tell me what is going on here?" I questioned, my hands forming into tight fists.

"Steve Mann was the younger brother of the gang member I took out a few years back," Chris murmured. "He got into some trouble with me after his brother died. He was granted bail maybe ten months ago, but he's not supposed to be in this area."

This was all a setup to get back at Chris. I frowned, my anger rising in me again.

Suddenly, a loud scream, followed by a loud bang, rang out from inside the storage garage. It cut the tension mounting between Chris and me and instantly, the officers, myself, and Chris ran in the direction it had come from.

Becca

"Stop screaming. I told you there is no one here who is going to save you." The words gritted through Jace's clenched teeth as he held the cold steel of the gun to my temple. "That was a warning shot. Another scream and I promise I will make this one count."

He covered my mouth with another strip of tape as he held my now-free hands over my head with one of his. He placed the gun back on the mattress beside me and continued trying hard to force his free hand into my pants.

Suddenly, a bang at the door pulled his attention away from me. He ripped his hand away, grabbed the gun, and got up off the mattress. I scurried away, balling myself up into the farthest corner I could get.

"Who's there?" he called out.

Another cling against the door was all I could hear.

"Everything okay in there?" I heard a voice call out.

Jace turned to look at me and held his finger up to his lips, signaling for me to be quiet. I squeezed my eyes shut tightly as the tears rolled down my cheeks.

"I heard a loud bang in there and am just checking to make sure you are all right?"

"Everything is fine," he barked out. "Just dropped something," Jace lied.

I glanced to the side doors and realized that Jace had forgotten to lock the roll door from the inside, which meant that whoever was on the outside could get in if they tried.

"You sure? Do you need any help?" the voice asked from the other side of the door.

I sat there praying someone lifted the door and noticed that Jace was now staring at me and turned to follow my line of sight. His eyes practically bulged out of his head when he noticed the door had not been secured. He took a few steps towards the door and did his best to lean over stuff that was in his way to reach the lock. I reached around, ripping the tape from my mouth, and let out a cry for help while Jace fought to make his way to the latch.

Jace turned in my direction and raised his gun just as the door was lifted.

"Drop your weapon."

A shot fired out. I rolled into a tight ball, and then a burning pain flooded my body. The last thing I remembered was falling off the mattress before I passed out.

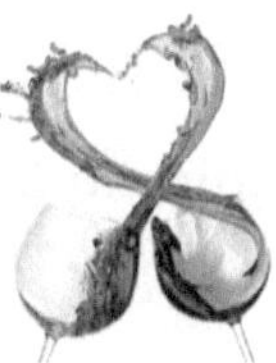

Bright lights shone into my eyes, and a dab of something cold and wet touched my forehead. Immediately, a surge of panic flew through me, and I flung my arms in front of me to stop whoever was there, a searing pain ripping through my arm causing me to stop.

"Whoa, whoa, calm down," I heard, as I felt firm hands grab hold of mine. "Shh, it's okay, you're okay."

I slowly calmed and allowed my view to come into focus. A doctor stood in front of me. "Becca, I'm Dr. Ava Moody, and you are at St. John's Hospital. We are treating you for a bullet graze to the arm and a few minor cuts and bruises," she said, taking a step closer to me and continuing to dab at my head.

"Bullet graze?" I slowly questioned as the once-cold liquid began to burn.

"Yes. Do you remember what happened?" she

questioned.

Images flashed through my mind as I remembered Jace turning and pointing a gun at me, followed by the loud shots that rang out. "A little."

"Well, let me finish getting you cleaned up, and then you can speak with the officers in charge," she said, continuing checking me over and dabbing at my face in spots.

A little while later, I lay in bed on my side with my eyes closed. I'd been kidnapped during the bomb threat at work, and Jace was now dead and I was alive, thank God. I heard the door to my room open, but I didn't bother to roll over. I felt the bed dip down on the opposite side and felt a large, warm hand rest gently on my leg.

I let out a deep breath and rolled over partially onto my back to see Grant sitting beside me. I placed my hand on his. My brother stood at the end of my bed.

"Thank God you are all right," Chris said, grabbing hold of my foot.

"We were worried about you," Grant continued.

"If it hadn't of been for you circling those charges on your credit card records and Grant here, we might not have found you," Chris continued.

I was overcome with emotion as I lay there looking back at both of them. My brother, who had placed

Grant in my path to protect me, and Grant, who had done nothing but his best to make sure I was safe, to make sure I felt safe, were both here by my side.

"I'm sorry I failed you, Bec," Grant said, gripping my leg.

I looked to my brother, who stood there shaking his head at Grant. "You didn't fail her. She's alive, isn't she?"

"Yeah, and scarred for life."

"Man, you are so stubborn." Grant turned and glared at Chris.

When I cleared my throat, Grant instantly hung his head, and Chris looked at me, shaking his.

I looked back at my brother. "Chris, can you get me a juice, please?" I asked before the two most important men in my life took a swing at one another. "Orange, if possible."

Chris looked at me and back to Grant then nodded. I had remembered a letter Grant had written to me after his troop had been attacked and how he had felt he had failed as a leader because three of his men would not be able to return home. He had stated how he wished it had been him who had died in the explosion. It had taken me a few weeks to figure out what to say to him after receiving that letter. I couldn't imagine how torn he must have been, or what it must have been like to be fighting that inner turmoil. Although, after all this time, I still had my doubts about what I had written to him. I feared my advice had been juvenile and probably didn't make him feel any better.

As soon as the door to my room had closed, I slowly sat up and pulled my legs into a criss-cross position. I scooted down towards Grant, trying hard not to use the arm that had been injured. I leaned in and wrapped my arms around his neck and held him. He didn't move, yet I stayed that way for a while, until I finally felt him wrap his arms around me. I even felt him place a kiss on my neck. We stayed like that for what felt like forever, until I placed my hand on his cheek.

"Do you remember the letter you wrote to me after your accident overseas?" I practically whispered.

Grant gave me a questioning look.

"The one you said you wished it had been you that had been killed when that IED went off?"

"How could I forget? I still live with that memory and that guilt every single day and will for my entire life."

I nodded in understanding. "I'm going to be honest with you. I never really knew how to answer you when I read that letter. I sat on it for two weeks, and what I wrote to you still probably didn't help you. I know you still carry that guilt with you that you failed people."

"Of course I do, but Becca, don't be ridiculous. You listened. You tried to help me. Of course, your words comforted me when I needed them most, like they always had."

I smiled and shook my head. "I think it's time that you let that guilt go, Grant. I want you to know that you didn't fail as a leader."

"Well, thank you, but I hate to tell you I did."

"But you didn't. If it had been you that night, then you wouldn't have been there to save me. You saved me."

Grant laughed. "I didn't save you, Becs."

"You did. You were the one who found those charges. You were the one who remembered you had put those cameras in."

Grant raised his head and looked into my eyes. "How did you know about that?"

"Jace. He told me that my boyfriend wouldn't be able to come and save me. That they had disconnected the cameras. So, if you had died that night, I would probably be dead now."

"Boyfriend? That's a joke." Grant huffed under his breath.

The door opened to my room, and Chris came striding in holding up an apple juice. "They were all out of orange," he said, cracking the lid of the bottle.

"Can you give us another minute?" I asked.

"Geez, no thanks for the juice, bro? What is this?" Chris said, laughing as he set the bottle down on the tray beside my bed and leaned in to kiss my forehead. "I'll go find out when we can get you out of here."

I watched as my brother walked across the room and left once again. I placed my hand under Grant's chin and lifted his head so he could look at me, resting my hand on his cheek.

"What?" he asked.

"I should have told you this a lot sooner, but I love you, Grant. I've loved you a long time now, and I realized it when Jace said those words to me."

He looked into my eyes and slowly brought his lips to mine. I closed my eyes as I felt his lips dance over mine, and I allowed my body to relax as he ran his muscular hands over me. When we parted, breathing hard, I rested my forehead against his.

"What is it?" he asked.

I looked into his eyes and smiled. "You. You are my saviour boy. You will always be my saviour boy. Truth be told, I would be thrilled to be called yours," I said, leaning in and meeting his lips. When I went to pull away, I felt his arms wrap around me and pull me in a little closer, deepening the kiss.

"Then I'm yours, Becca Scott."

Epilogue

Becca

I stood in the little room looking at myself in the mirror. I could feel my stomach flip as I looked over myself once more, making sure that every strand of hair was perfectly in place, that my makeup was on perfectly. I glanced to my arm, at the scar that stood out prominently. I had never been so nervous, yet I had no idea why because I had never been so sure of something in my life.

I picked up my bouquet that sat on the side table and looked down at the tightly closed pink roses. I brought them up to my nose and inhaled deeply, relishing in their scent. I then ran my hand down the silky satin of my dress, smoothing out any wrinkles, and smiled to myself.

I swallowed hard and brushed away a tear that had slipped down my cheek, then smiled to myself when I heard a soft knock on the door. It was time.

I pulled the door open to see my dad standing there looking as handsome as ever in his suit.

"You ready?" he questioned, holding his arm out for me to slide my arm through.

I nodded, smiled, and bit my lower lip. He kissed me on the cheek, then rested his warm hand over mine. "Let's go, shall we?"

I allowed memories to run through my mind while we walked down the hall. Memories of the years when we were kids, then the years I had written to Grant while he had been overseas. Then the memories of the last year and half ran through my mind, each one of them producing a smile.

Finally, we stood outside of The Merlot Room at Braun Ranch Vineyards. I could hear many voices on the other side of the door, and then a piano played, and the voices quieted.

"You sure you are ready?" my father said, tapping his large hand on mine. I looked up into my father's eyes and smiled.

"I've never been so sure of anything in my entire life," I whispered, swallowing hard.

"All right then," he said, leaning in to kiss me on the cheek.

I lowered my head as the doors opened, and when I felt myself take that first step with my father at my side, I looked up and all I saw was Grant, standing there in his suit staring back at me. I couldn't wait to get to him, to say I do and become Mrs. Becca Moore.

A Note from the Author

Dear Readers,

I would like to thank you for taking the time to read *Saviour Boy*. I hope you enjoyed Grant and Becca's story. If you did, I would love it if you would drop me a review. Reviews are so important and really help me; plus I love to hear what my readers think.

If you loved Saviour Boy make sure to read The Boy Under the Gazebo, the second book in the Forever Boys Series.

About the Author

S.L. Sterling had been an avid reader since she was a child, often found getting lost in books. Today if she isn't writing or plotting, she can be found buried in a romance novel. S.L. Sterling lives with her husband and dog in Northern Ontario.

If you'd like to stay up to date with me sign up for my Newsletter and join my reader group, Sterling's Silver Sapphires.

Or

Visit my Website

Other Titles by S.L. Sterling

It Was Always You

On A Silent Night

Bad Company

Back to You this Christmas

Fireside Love

Holiday Wishes

The Greatest Gift

Into the Sunset

Doctor Desire

The Malone Brother Series

A Kiss Beneath the Stars

In Your Arms

His to Hold

Finding Forever with You

Vegas MMA

Dagger

KB Worlds: Everyday Heroes

Constraint